NATURE HUNT

BEWILD__NG · PUZZLES · OF · THE · ANIMAL · KINGDOM

PHILIP · BLYTHE

For Cher
— PB

Little Hare Books
4/21 Mary Street, Surry Hills
NSW 2010 AUSTRALIA
www.littleharebooks.com

National Library of Australia
Cataloguing-in-Publication entry

Blythe, Philip.
Nature Hunt

For children.
ISBN 1 877003 82 4 (pbk.).

1. Picture puzzles - Juvenile literature. 2. Maze puzzles -
Juvenile literature. 3. Animals - Juvenile literature.
I. Title.

793.73

Designed by Serious Business
Produced by Phoenix Offset, Hong Kong
Printed in China

5 4 3 2 1

From a very early age I was fascinated by life—the kind that may exist on other planets! But the more I learned about life here on Earth, the more I realised that there is an endless variety of fascinating creatures right here.

Nature Hunt is a look at the hidden world of the animal kingdom. For many creatures, whether hunter or hunted, survival depends on not being seen—or not being seen as they really are! Some animals hide, some develop wonderful patterns to blend in to their surroundings, and others try to look bigger or more ferocious than they actually are in order to scare away predators.

Now you, too, can join the nature hunt, as you solve the puzzles of these 12 very different environments. Remember to stay alert! Hidden dangers are lurking in many of these scenes… Whether you are guiding a fish through a maze of coral, playing seek-and-find with a jungle full of monkeys, or looking for a bird's-eye view of a worm, you will always need a keen eye.

Finally, behind all of the worlds depicted here lie some strange but true facts—you can find them following the final puzzle, just before the solutions.

GRIZZLY BEARS

Flipping and flapping fish; growling and grasping grizzlies. While the bears are trying to catch their lunch, 10 crayfish slip through. Can you spot them all?

BIRDS OF THE AIR

All the birds of the air and more;
there's two of each—except for one.
Which is the single bird? And which
is the early bird that caught the worm?

THE SECRET GARDEN

A blaze of colour, a wealth of
shapes and, trying to remain
unseen, 15 very different creatures.
Can you find them all before
they disappear?

DESERT EYES

Steely eyes and sharp ears help the
coyote search for food—but the
14 jackrabbits are good at hiding
in shadows. Who'll be the first to
find them: you, the coyote—or
the four hidden snakes?

DANGERS IN THE DEEP

There are 19 jellyfish swimming
this way and that, in and out and
between sharks, rays and whales.
Can you see them all?
(One is very hard to spot!)

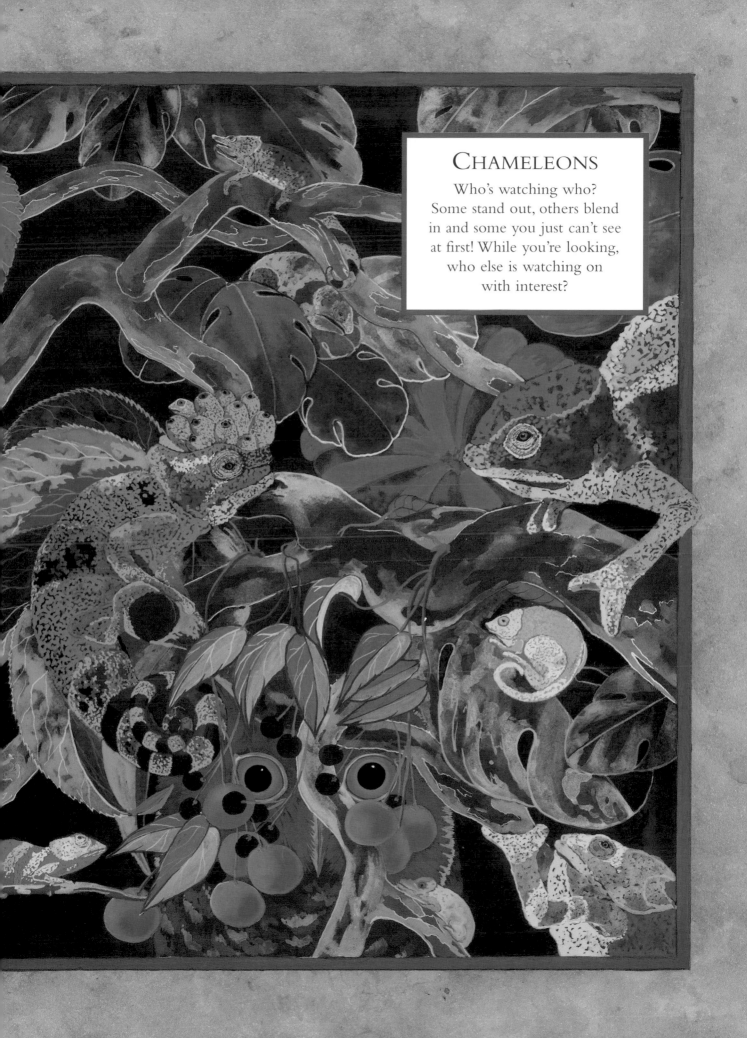

CHAMELEONS

Who's watching who?
Some stand out, others blend
in and some you just can't see
at first! While you're looking,
who else is watching on
with interest?

SCUTTLING CRABS

Clickety snappity clack! The crabs scuttle through the seaweed to the ocean, but one's caught up and can't escape. Who is caught? And where are the five fish hiding?

RAINFOREST

Slow and steady, one branch at a time. Can you help the sloth reach the tasty leaves opposite? You must keep to the path, and there's no jumping allowed—but the 3D path winds round and round, so concentration is a must!

MOUNTAIN PATH

Wandering woollies and a path that goes every way but up! Can you help find the best way to the top, starting from the bottom? Then round up all 19 sheep—and see if you can find a twentieth hidden in the landscape!

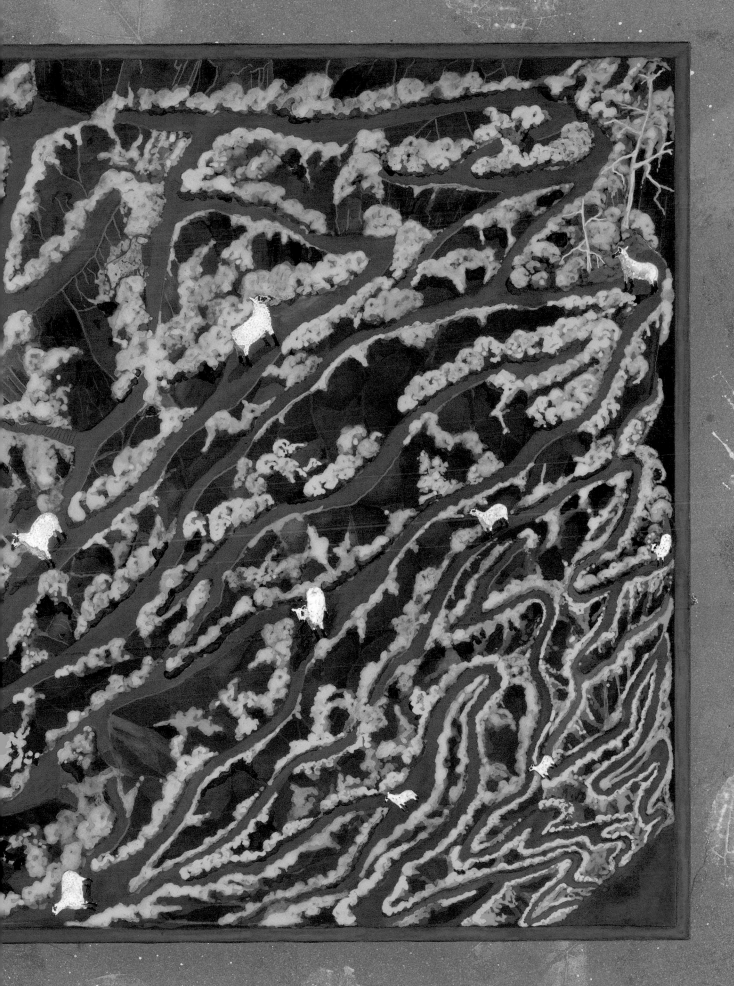

TRUNKS AND TAILS

A trail of trunks and tails.
This young egret wants to join
the others in the middle,
but cannot fly. The only path
is by way of trunks and tails.
Don't slip or you'll get
very, very wet!

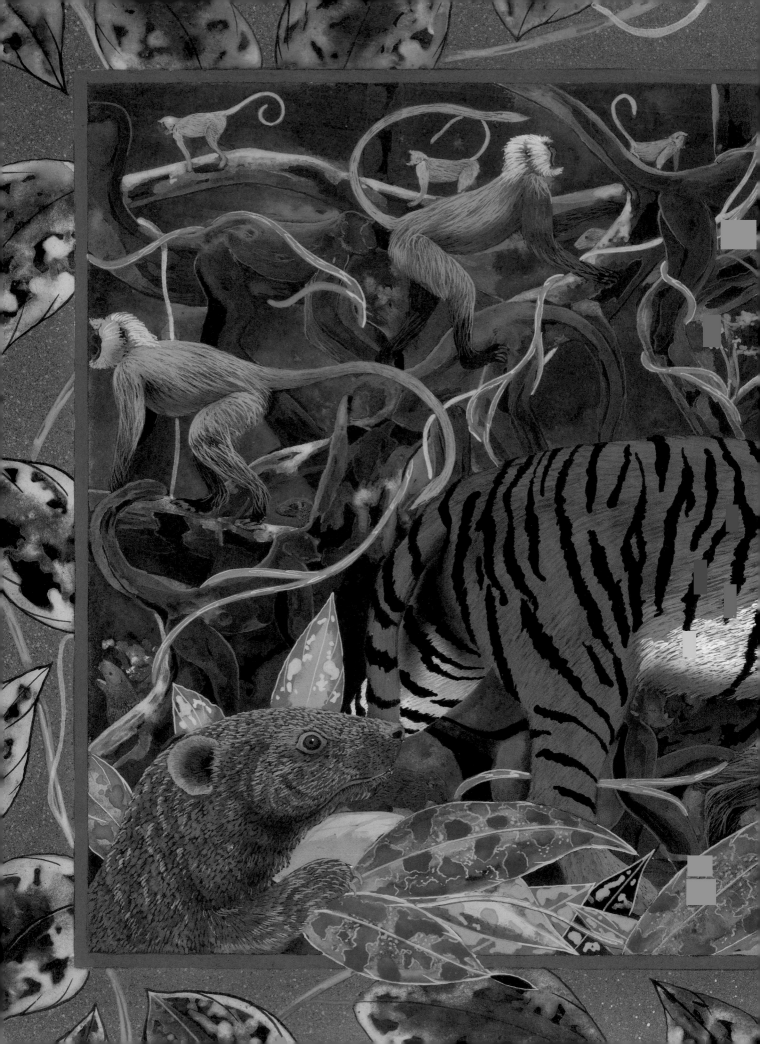

TIGER IN THE JUNGLE

When the tiger takes a stroll the
jungle turns to hush and still.
Can you see all 18 monkeys
and half as many mongooses
in the picture?

WRECK ON THE REEF

Swim with the angelfish between
the beds of coral to find a path that
leads to the safety of the wreck.
Watch out for the four large
coral trout and five sleeping sharks.
Are there any other dangers?

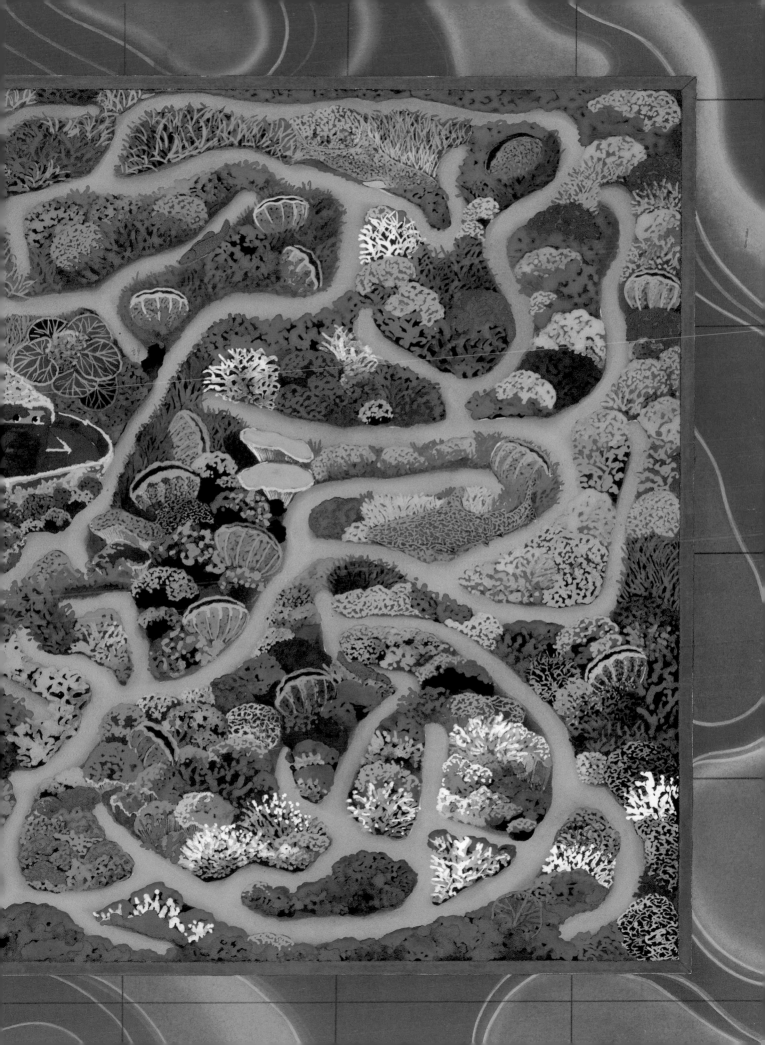

GRIZZLY BEARS

The grizzly bear gets its name from its silver-tipped brown fur, which gives it a "grizzled" look. During a mild winter, these bears sometimes break their hibernation to search for food—which, amazingly, is mostly vegetarian!

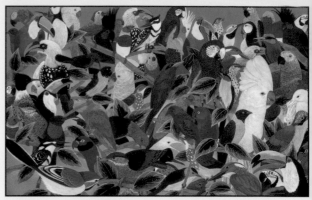

BIRDS OF THE AIR

The Arctic tern travels from pole to pole, flying more than 35 000 km in a single year. The sooty tern, meanwhile, remains in the air for 3 years or more before returning to land to breed. During this time it never lands; it even sleeps on the wing!

THE SECRET GARDEN

In order to be called an insect, a creature must have three body parts—a head, thorax and abdomen; six jointed legs; two antennae; and an outside skeleton.

DESERT EYES

A coyote walks on its toes, making its tracks very easy to identify. Known as the Desert Wolf, coyotes actually belong to the order Carnivora and family Canidae—dogs, in plain English!

DANGERS IN THE DEEP

Jellyfish have no bones, head, brain, heart, eyes or ears, and are not even fish—but they can sting! They are related to corals and sea anemones, and drift with the ocean currents, stinging and feeding.

CHAMELEONS

A chameleon's eyes can rotate independently, giving it a 360-degree view without even needing to turn its head! The word chameleon is derived from the ancient Greek for "ground lion".

SCUTTLING CRABS

Legend has it that the Sally Lightfoot crab was named after a nineteenth-century dancer who wore a red dress. But its Latin name best sums up this little Galapagos Island scavenger's lifestyle: *Graspus graspus*!

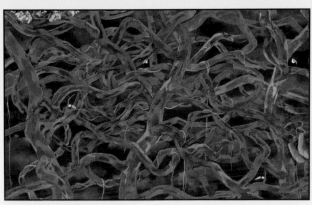

RAINFOREST

All sloths have three toes on their feet, but two-toed sloths are so-called because they have only two claws on their hands. The sloth may be slow, but it's not harmless; if threatened it can lash out with huge sharp claws and bite with its teeth.

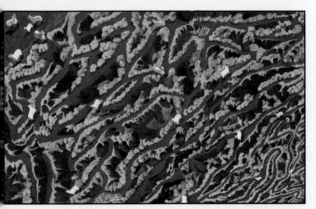

MOUNTAIN PATH

Sheep grow two teeth a year until they have eight—and they are all in the lower jaw. That's not many teeth for an animal whose stomach has four compartments to fill!

TRUNKS AND TAILS

Elephants sleep standing upright! African elephants have larger bodies, bigger ears, less bumpy foreheads, and longer tusks than Asian elephants. Asian elephants have five toes on their front feet and four on their hind feet; African elephants have four toes on their front feet and three on their hind feet.

TIGER IN THE JUNGLE

Tigers see six times as well as humans in the dark, but the big cats' daytime vision is worse than ours. The largest of the cat family, a tiger's stripes are as individual as a fingerprint, with no two tigers having the same striped pattern.

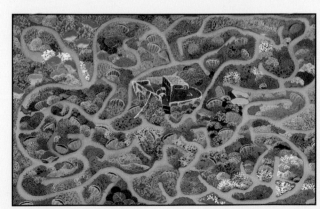

WRECK ON THE REEF

Coral is a living organism composed of tiny fragile animals called coral polyps. Although the rate of growth is very slow—less than 2 cm a year—these polyps are responsible for building the world's largest biological structure: the Great Barrier Reef in Australia!

SOLUTIONS

BIRDS OF THE AIR

DESERT EYES

GRIZZLY BEARS

THE SECRET GARDEN

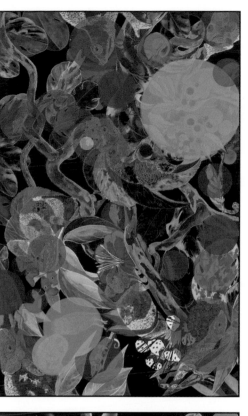

CHAMELEONS

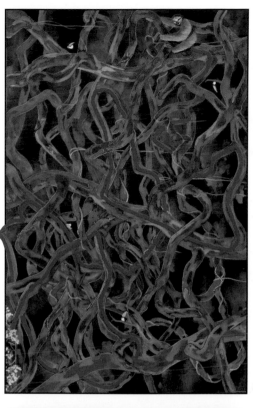

RAINFOREST

DANGERS IN THE DEEP

SCUTTLING CRABS

Trunks and Tails

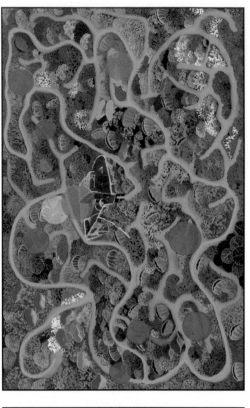

Wreck on the Reef

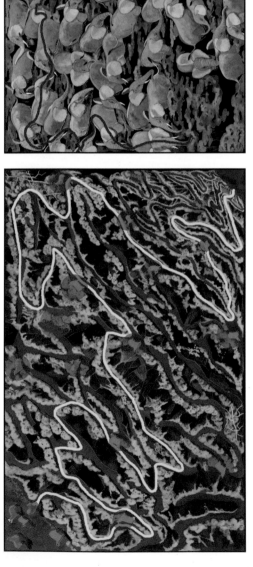

Mountain Path

Tiger in the Jungle